CAN
NEW DOV
LEAR

D0475837

CANTERBURY COLLEGE
NEW DOVER ROAD
CANTERBURY CT1 3AJ
LIBRARY
CLASS No. 372.216 BRA
ECK.
BOOK No. 51308

This book introduces young children to the names of basic shapes and colours.

Each page is illustrated using bold, colourful pictures of objects that children will enjoy recognising and naming. There are simple questions to encourage discussion and give practice in counting and colour and shape recognition.

Available in Series 921

*† **a for apple**

*† **let's count**

* **what is the time?**

* **shapes and colours**

Also available in square format Series S808 *and* † *as* Ladybird Teaching Friezes

First edition

Published by Ladybird Books Ltd Loughborough Leicestershire UK
Ladybird Books Inc Auburn Maine 04210 USA

© LADYBIRD BOOKS LTD MCMXCII

All rights reserved. No part of this publication may be reproduced, stored in a retrieval system, or transmitted in any form or by any means, electronic, mechanical, photocopying, recording or otherwise, without the prior consent of the copyright owner.

Printed in England (3)

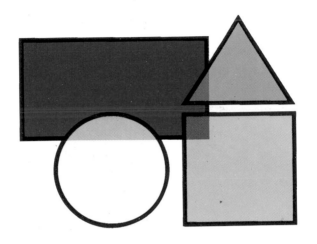

shapes
and
colours

written by LYNNE BRADBURY
illustrated by LYNN N GRUNDY

Ladybird Books

This shape is called a **circle**.

Circles go round and round.
They have no corners.

A wheel is a **circle** shape.

How many wheels can you count on this page?

Do you know some more **circle** shapes?

The colour of this circle is called **red**.

There are lots of different **reds**.

Here are some **red** things.

Do you know what they are?

This shape is called a **square**.

Squares have four sides the same length and four corners.

Some of these houses and windows are **square** shapes.

How many **squares** can you count on this page?

Do you know some more **square** shapes?

The elephant has painted this square a colour called **blue**.

There are lots of different **blues**.

Which things here are **blue**?

What colour is the kite?

This shape is called a **triangle**.

Triangles have three sides and three corners.

The three sides of a **triangle**
are not always the same length.

How many **triangles** can you
count on this page?

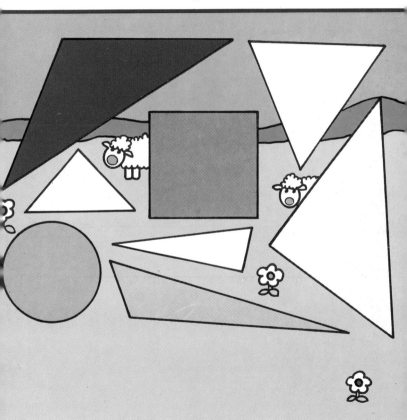

The colour of this triangle
is called **yellow**.

There are lots of different
yellows.

Can you name these things?

Do you know any other **yellow** things?

This shape is called
a **rectangle**.

Rectangles have four corners
and four sides. Two sides are
long and two sides are short.

Rectangles can be fat, thin,
long or short.

How many **rectangles** are there
on this page?

Which **rectangle** is yellow?

The boy is painting the rectangle **blue**. The girl is painting it **yellow**.

Blue and **yellow** mixed together make a colour called **green**.

There are different **greens**.

What are these **green** things called?

The monkeys have found some **red** paint and some **yellow** paint.

When they mix them together it makes a colour called **orange**.

What have the monkeys painted
orange?

The cat has some **blue** paint.
The dog has some **red** paint.

Red and **blue** mixed together
make a colour called **purple**.

Name the shapes on this page.

Which shapes are coloured **purple**?

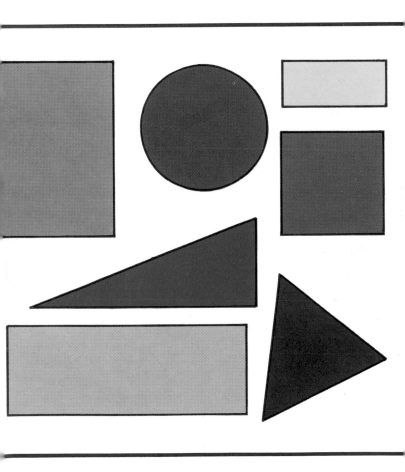

Everything on these pages is
black and **white**.

The snowman has a **black** hat.
The rabbit is **white**.

Talk about these **black** and **white** things.

Do you know their names?

If **black** and **white** are mixed together, they make a colour called **grey**.

What are these **grey** animals called?

If a little bit of **red** is mixed together with **white**, it makes a colour called **pink**.

What are these **pink** things?